Mother Rabbit Knew

written by Carolyn Koster Yost

illustrated by Katherine W. Gardner

"With your wisdom you made them all."—Psalm 104:24

Library of Congress Catalog Card No. 88-63568
© 1989, The STANDARD PUBLISHING Company, Cincinnati, Ohio
Division of STANDEX INTERNATIONAL Corporation. Printed in U.S.A.

Mother Rabbit came hopping through the backyard of Michael's house, hippity-hop, hippity-hop.

She stopped every so often and smelled the air, wiggling her little nose, wiggly-wig, wiggly-wig.

Mother Rabbit was looking for a very special place.

God knew why, and Mother Rabbit
knew why. Do you know why?

She hopped up a little hill near Michael's back door, hippity-hop, hippity-hop.

Then she stopped and wiggled her nose extra hard, wiggly-wig, wiggly-wig.

Her long ears flicked up and down, flickity-flick, flickity-flick.

Then Mother Rabbit began kicking
her long back legs into the grass and
dirt, making a little hole, kickity-kick,
kickity-kick.

She pulled fur from her chest and pu
it in the little hole. Finally, she covere
everything up with dried grass.

God knew why, and Mother Rabbit knew why. Do you know why?

Every night for two whole weeks, Mother Rabbit came back to the little hole she'd made.

During the day, she hid in the bushes nearby, dozing and watching the little hole.

God knew why, and Mother Rabbit knew why. Do you know why?

Meanwhile, the grass in the yard grew longer. One day Michael's dad said, "Spring is here. It's time to mow the grass."

Dad started the lawn mower, and Michael covered his ears at the loud sound, roar-roar, roar-roar.

Michael's dad mowed right over the place where Mother Rabbit had kicked grass and dirt, roar-roar, roar-roar. Now the grass was short around the little hole.

But Michael didn't see the little hole. Neither did his dad, because it was covered up with dried grass.

Mother Rabbit had heard the lawn mower. Over in the bushes, her little nose wiggled, wiggly-wig, wiggly-wig. Her long ears flicked up and down, flickity-flick, flickity-flick. Her heart thumped with fear, thumpity-thump, thumpity-thump.

God knew why, and Mother Rabbit
knew why. Do you know why?

A few days later, Michael saw some fur mixed in with the dried grass.

"What's this?" he asked his dad.

"Why, it's rabbit fur," said Dad.

Carefully Dad lifted up a handful of dried grass. Michael saw more loose fur.

When Dad lifted the fur, Michael peeked into the hole. He saw a baby rabbit curled up. Its little ears were lying flat along its back. Its little heart was beating hard, thumpity-thump, thumpity-thump.

"There are probably more babies too, but we'll just let them alone," Dad said.

He carefully put the fur back in the hole and covered everything up with the dried grass. Then Michael and Dad went into the house.

During the night, Mother Rabbit came back to the hole. She began pushing her babies. Soon they all jumped up out of the hole, hopped across the yard, and went into the bushes.

God knew why, and Mother Rabbit
knew why. Do you know why?

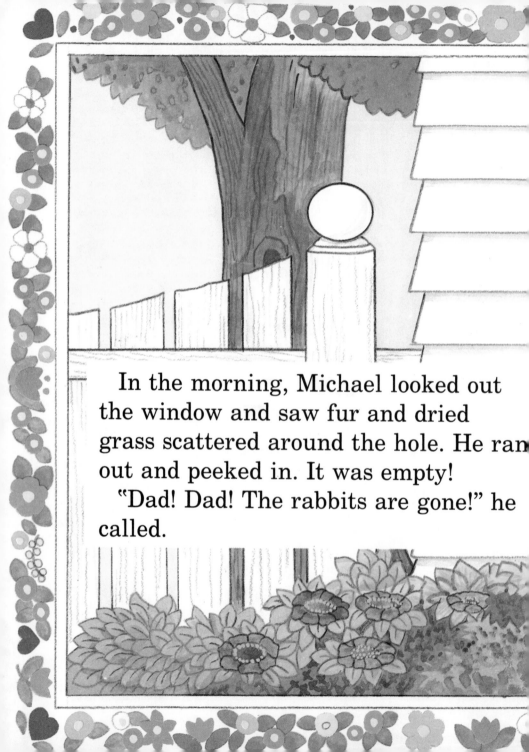

In the morning, Michael looked out the window and saw fur and dried grass scattered around the hole. He ran out and peeked in. It was empty!

"Dad! Dad! The rabbits are gone!" he called.

Over in the bushes, Mother Rabbit showed her babies how to sit very still, almost as still as stones.

The babies did as their mother wanted and sat still in the bushes. Each one looked very much like a stone.

God knew why, and Mother Rabbit knew why. Do you know why?